The Sandcastle

Mick Gowar & Lesley Harker

FRANKLIN WATTS
LONDON•SYDNEY

The sun was hot, the sky was blue,
the sea was calm –
and Mum and Dad
were fast asleep.

"Let's make a sandcastle," said Jack.
"We'll make it round." Jack drew the shape in the sand.
"Start digging!" said Jack.

The castle grew and grew.
"Is it finished yet?" I asked.
"Almost," said Jack.

"All it needs is something oblong
to make a bridge – like that piece of wood."
I fetched it.
    "That's the one!" said Jack.

"Is it finished now?" I asked.

"Nearly," said Jack.

"All it needs is two flags for the towers.
Our handkerchiefs will do."

Jack tied his hankie to an ice cream stick. I folded mine over. "Just right!" said Jack. "Perfect!" said Jack.

and one is a triangle.

Dad woke up. "It's too close to the sea," he said. "The waves will wash it all away."

"Not my castle," said Jack. "My castle has thick walls, and a bridge, and towers, and flags on flag-poles."

He sat on top of the castle. The waves lapped around the castle. "Help!" shouted Jack. "The bridge has been washed away – get something oblong."

"One of the towers has fallen down."

"My flag's been washed away –
quick get something square!"

"And something long and thin..."
"Too late!"

"Never mind," said Dad.

"You can build another one tomorrow."

"And have it washed away again?" said Jack.

"Not me!"

If at first you don't succeed ... build with bricks!

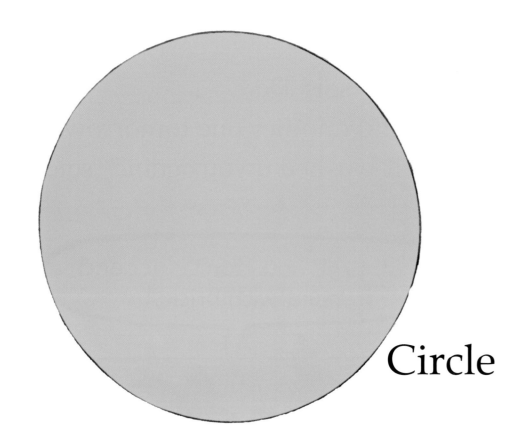

Circle

Oblong

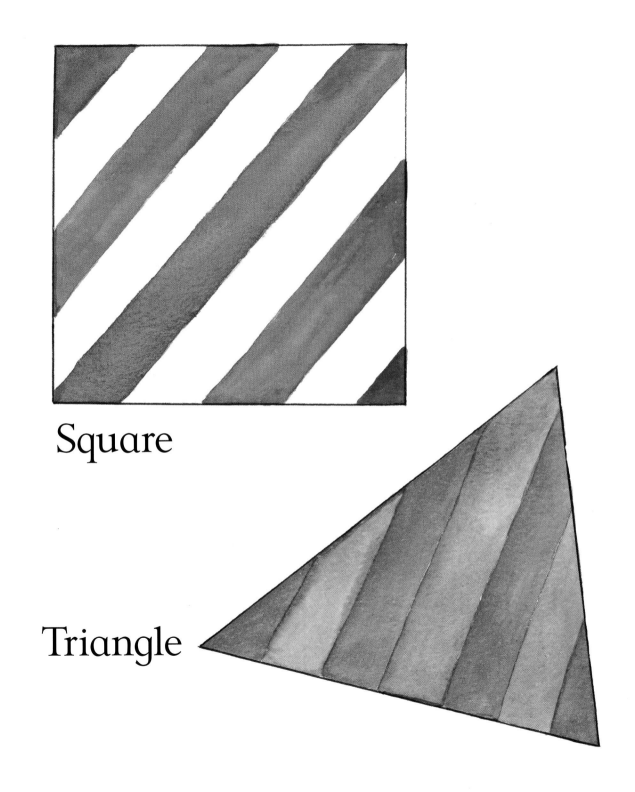

Square

Triangle

Sharing books with your child

Me and My World are a range of books for you to share with your child. Together you can look at the pictures and talk about the subject or story. Listening, looking and talking are the first vital stages in children's reading development, and lay the early foundation for good reading habits.

Talking about the pictures is the first step in involving children in the pages of a book, especially if the subject or story can be related to their own familiar world. When children can relate the matter in the book to their own experience, this can be used as a starting point for introducing new knowledge, whether it is counting, getting to know colours or finding out how other people live.

Gradually children will develop their listening and concentration skills as well as a sense of what a book is. Soon they will learn how a book works: that you turn the pages from right to left, and read the story from left to right on a double page. They start to realize that the black marks on the page have a meaning and that they relate to the pictures. Once children have grasped these basic essentials they will develop strategies for "decoding" the text such as matching words and pictures, and recognising the rhythm of the language in order to predict what comes next. Soon they will start to take on the role of an independent reader, handling and looking at books even if they can't yet read the words.

Most important of all, children should realize that books are a source of pleasure. This stems from your reading sessions which are times of mutual enjoyment and shared experience. It is then that children find the key to becoming real readers.

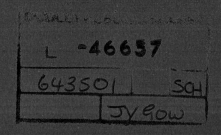
This edition 2003

Franklin Watts
96 Leonard Street,
London EC2A 4XD

Franklin Watts Australia
45-51 Huntley Street
Alexandria NSW 2015

ISBN 0 7496 4913 5

A CIP catalogue record for this book is available from the British Library
Dewey Classification 516

First published as *Jack and Me and the Seaside* in the Early Worms series

Printed in Belgium

Consultant advice: Sue Robson and Alison Kelly,
Senior Lecturers in Education,
Faculty of Education, Early Childhood Centre,
Roehampton Institute, London.